Blind Witness

Three American Operas

Blind Witness

Three American Operas

Libretti by Charles Bernstein

Music by Ben Yarmolinsky

Factory School, 2008
Queens, NYC

Blind Witness
Three American Operas

Libretti by Charles Bernstein

Music by Ben Yarmolinsky

PS3577
Factory School
Queens, New York

ISBN 978-1-60001-993-7 (paper)
ISBN 978-1-60001-984-5 (cloth)

Cover art: Susan Bee, *Spirits of '76*, 1998,
oil and collage on linen, 62 x 50" (detail).

Blind Witness News was first published in *Ploughshares*, vol. 17, no. 1, 1991.
The Subject was first published by Meow Press in 1995.
The Lenny Paschen Show was published as *Abacus* #86, 1994.

Recordings of these operas are available at
http://writing.upenn.edu/pennsound/x/Yarmolinsky.html

Factory School is a learning and production collective engaged in action
research, multiple-media arts, publishing, and community service.
For more information please visit factoryschool.org.

Contents

Preface

Ben Yarmolinsky

At the end of the summer of 1990, I received a call from Grethe Holby, the artistic director of American Opera Projects. She asked me if I would be interested in writing a new opera. The previous spring I had submitted a cassette of songs to AOP in response to an advertisement, and apparently they liked what they heard. I said that I would be thrilled to write a new opera, and began to think about a subject. Since my early twenties I had toyed with the idea of writing a musical theater piece based on a television news broadcast, and I suggested that as the theme. She accepted.

The next question was who would write the libretto. With only about three months until the scheduled performance, I thought I'd better farm the job out. I remembered the name of Charles Bernstein. The summer before in Tangier, my friend Rodrigo Rey Rosa had mentioned him to me as the leader of the L=A=N=G=U=A=G=E poetry movement—a movement about which I knew nothing. Still, it sounded intriguing, and I knew that Charles lived in New York. So, I looked up all the Charles Bernsteins in the phone book and hit on the right one after a few tries.

Charles was immediately receptive to the idea of writing the libretto and we met a few days later to talk it over. By the end of our first meeting we had decided on a cast of four singers: Jack James & Jill Johns — anchorman and woman respectively, Jane Jones — weatherwoman, and John Jacks — sportscaster. We also decided on a four-part format of International News, Local News, Weather and Sports. My original title for the piece was "News Songs," but Charles felt that this title was — in his words — "too bland." I deferred to his judgment.

The first part that I composed was Jill's aria "Against the menace." The words called forth a music that was operatic, dark, and expressive. The rest of the libretto elicited many different styles of music—so many that *The New York Times* critic called the score "wildly eclectic."

Early on I decided to score the piece for two electric keyboards. There was no piano in the performance space, and I knew that I wanted a musical accompaniment that was primarily harmonic and rhythmic, but that had some variety of timbre.

The premiere of *Blind Witness News* took place on December 3, 1990, at the American Opera Project's Blue Door Studio at 463 Broome Street in Soho. The cast included Rhondi Charlston, James Javore, Susanna Guzman, and Lynn Randolph. The late Robert Black conducted. Grethe Barrett Holby directed.

In December of 2005, Cantiamo Opera staged a revival of *Blind Witness News*. For these four performances Charles and I collaborated on a new segment based on the national news, including a new aria for the anchorman. I also revised the original score and arranged it for solo piano accompaniment. The performers were Deborah Karpel, Nathan Resika, Leandra Ramm, and Aram Tchobanian. Ishmael Wallace was the pianist/musical director.

In the summer of '92, Charles and I embarked on a companion piece to *Blind Witness News*, again under the sponsorship of AOP and Holby. We both realized that the inevitable follow-up to an operatic parody of the evening news would have to be an operatic parody of a late night television talk show. Thus began *The Lenny Paschen Show*. The concept was that our host, Lenny, would be an outrageous comedian in the mold of Lenny Bruce, and that he would be giving his last performance—his show having been cancelled by the network. His guests would include three celebrity types: a young ambitious pop star, Monica Moolah, a country & western singer, Paul Evangeline, and an aging diva, Maria Aquavita. As with *Blind Witness News*, we would follow the format of our television model scrupulously, including theme music, announcer, opening monologue, commercial breaks, and so on. The content would be Charles' typical mish-mash of sense and nonsense.

The libretto was done by June and I took it with me to Normandy and Paris where I worked on it in July and August and finished it in New York in the fall.

In an effort to make a score that sounded like television music, and, equally important, in an effort to save money, I scored the accompaniment for a synthesized band of saxophone, guitar, keyboard, bass, and percussion. The piece was performed to a prerecorded computer-generated accompaniment. The musical styles here are more consistent although there is still considerable variety. The prerecorded accompaniment demanded a very precise performance from the singers.

A staged reading of *The Lenny Paschen Show* took place in November of '92, again produced by American Opera Projects at 463 Broome St. The cast included Larry Adams, Darryn Zimmer, Jeff Reynolds and Jane Shaulis. John Yaffé was the conductor. Holby directed.

The genesis of our second opera, *The Subject*, was different from that of the other two. Nobody asked for it. For some reason I decided that an opera based on a psychoanalytic session would be a bright idea. Just as in the news and talk show formats, a psychoanalytic session has a ticking clock and an inherent real-time structure. It may be filled with almost any verbal content. In discussing this idea Charles and I agreed that it would be a fifty-minute hour (this was before pychotherapists decided to make their sessions 45 minutes long), which would include the recounting of a dream, a scheduling duet, psychiatric advice, and other familiar set pieces.

In homage to Brecht and Weill we named our "subject" Jenny Midnight. Her analyst, a conventional Freudian, was named Dr. Boris Frame (of the Frame Institute). We also decided that there would be an intervention by a second psychiatrist of the non-Freudian, pharmacological and behaviorist persuasion, named Daemon Dudley, and that the two would fight over the analysand. Thus, the opera would become a sort of theater of ideas, in which the two doctors sing about their opposing philosophies.

The character of the music for *The Subject* is lyrical and intimate. It is scored for solo piano accompaniment.

This opera was composed in Normandy in the summer of 1991. Again, I finished the work in the fall in New York.

The premiere performance was given at a private home on the Upper East Side of Manhattan in February of 1992. The role of Jenny Midnight was sung by Carla Wood, Boris Frame by Stephen Kalm, and Dr. Dudley by Tom Bogdan. Elizabeth Rodgers was the pianist. The City Opera of New York chose *The Subject* as an alternate for its Vox 2004 reading series, but the work was not performed by them.

These three operas (if they are operas) from the early 1990s represent my ideas about how contemporary American English ought to be sung. There is a consistent attempt in the text-setting to follow the rhythms and cadences of our language as it is spoken. Although I collaborated on the scenarios, suggested some verse forms, occasionally asked for slight changes to the original text, and sometimes asked for a second verse or a refrain, ultimately, the music was evoked by the words.

Blind Witness News

Cast

Jack James — Anchor Man — Baritone

Jill Johns — Anchor Woman — Soprano

Jane Jones — Weather — Mezzo-Soprano

John Jacks — Sports — Tenor

Scene I – International

Opening Theme

Jack & Jill: This is the Blind Witness News
With the Blind Witness news team

Jill: I'm Jill Johns

Jack: I'm Jack James

Jack & Jill: & this is the news
Blind Witness News, Blind Witness news, Blind Witness news.
What you see is what you got
What you get is what we saw

Jack: I'm Jack James

Jill: I'm Jill Johns

Jack: I'm Jack James

Jill: I'm Jill Johns

Jack & Jill: I'm Jack Jack Jack Jack Jack Jack Jack Jack James
I'm Jill Jill Jill Jill Jill Jill Jill Johns

Jack: I'm Jack James

Jill: I'm Jill Johns

Jack & Jill: & this is the news

Blind Witness News, Blind Witness News
Blind Witness News.

We show what we've got
You've got what we show
Take it or leave it, slip, slide, or blow

Jill: Tonight's top story is war.

Jack: Holy war in the North
Holy war in the East
Holy war in the West
Victory, victory soon to be ours

Jill: Victory, victory soon to be ours

Jack & Jill: Victory, victory, war, war holy war

Jack: Holy war in the North
Holy war in the East
Holy war in the West
Victory, victory soon to be ours

Jill: Victory, victory soon to be ours

Jack & Jill: Victory, victory, war, war, holy war

This is the Blind Witness News
With the Blind Witness News team

Jill: I'm Jill Johns with Jack James
Jack: I'm Jack James with Jill Johns

Jack & Jill: Jane Jones will be joining us with weather
John Jacks will be joining us with sports
Jane Jones will be joining us with weather
John Jacks will be joining us with sports

Jack: I'm Jack James

Jill: I'm Jill Johns

Jack & Jill: & this is the news,
Blind Witness News, Blind Witness News,
Blind Witness News.

We show what we've got
You've got what we show
We show what we've got
You've got what we show.

Don't go away, don't go away, don't go away
Stay with us
Don't go away, don't go away, don't go away
Stay right there
Stay with us, don't go away.

Jill: Tonight's top story is war.

Against the menace foreign
Menace at home
Menace that tears and gnaws
Menace no solace obscures

Except to pluck it out
No means to bail
But tell tale told

Tell again
Outbend the song

Menace inside
Menace that crawls and sprawls
Menace no solace obscures

Except to pluck it out
Outbend the song
Tears and gnaws
Unjarred too long
In wet and tattered fray

Who felt too far, or lay too near
And falling felt astounding blow
'Gainst all that slay
In combat's boulevards,
What heart no longer plays
No longer pays.

Against the menace foreign
Menace at home
Menace no solace obscures

Except to pluck it out
Except to pluck it out
Except to pluck it out

No more delayed,
Rejoin a polity
No more delayed
No more delayed.

Jack & Jill: Don't go away, don't go away, don't go away
Stay with us.
Don't go away, don't go away, don't go away
Stay right there.
Stay with us, don't go away.
We'll be right back.

Scene II – National

Jack: Coming up

Jill: Coming up

Jack & Jill: Income Gap Becomes Crater
We'll come back, we'll come back, we'll come back to that
Good motivation to get rich

Jill: We've got polls

Jack: We've got polls

Jack & Jill: We've got polls, we've got polls, we've got polls

Jack: Race called a factor, Jill

Jill: Not race, Jack, class

Jack: A lot of class and it's a race to get us back on track

Jack & Jill: Coming up, coming up, coming up

Jack & Jill: We'll come back, we'll come back, we'll come back to that

Jill: Now Jack's up
With some bluesy reflections
In a segment we call
"Behind the News"
Jack James in his own voice
Jack James in
"Behind the Blind"

Jack: Thanks, Jill
       Jill, thanks
       Thanks so much, Jill
       Really, you know, thanks
       Sometimes in the business, well, Jill
       Sometimes in this business
       You feel there's no you, you know
       No me, you know
       No me or you there
       No there there
       Thanks, Jill, really, you know
       So here's my me, my my
       Thanks, really thanks, Jill
       OK, here you go —
       A small departure, something I want you all to know

Jack's Blues

When you hit rock bottom, there's no further down you can go
When you reach the bottom, there's no further down you can go
When you stumble once and start to fall
Your friends gone out, won't take your call
When you smack that rock, you sink down deep in a hole.

Well, you lose your money, lose your wedding band
Yes, you lose your money, lose your wedding band
Just when you think — win, place or show
Then in a wink, no place to go,
No place to go, nobody to understand

They take your suits and take your ties
And give you a bottle of gin

Then they take your buttons and needles too
And don't leave a single pin
Yesterday's flash in the pan, big-time anchorman
Today in lights, tomorrow oblivion.

Now my heart's on my sleeve, I'd do anything to please
Take the shirt off my back, a Calvin Klein cotton chemise
Oh, I gave you all I have to give, too young to die, afraid to live
I've nothing left, I'm falling down on my knees, Jeeze!
Can you feel my pain? It's rising by degrees!

Scene III – Local

Jack: A Fargo man damaged a porch
      Punched an opening through
      Stuck his hand in it
      Made a one-foot hole

Jill: A Plymouth woman drowned
      Fell through the ground and drowned
      Just went into the water
      When she was told she hadn't oughta
      & drowned

Jack: A Chittawaga boy
      Stole a bike
      Rather than hike
      Threw the fight
      Played some drums
      Pummeled a nun
      Tanked up on rum
      And away he run

Jill: A couple from Daffy-on-Mill
      Went up Ambiguity Hill
      To ditch a pail of toxins
      The guy fell down
      Broke his frown
      The girl came tumbling after

Jack: That's local and I'm Jack James with Jill Johns

Jill: Jill Johns with Jack James

Jack: That's local and I'm Jack James with Jill Johns

Jill: Jill Johns with Jack James

Jack: A deranged man ravished a flag
       Punched an opening through
       Stuck his pie in it
       Ate it quite in view

Jill: An oft-lost lady cried
       Fell to the ground and died
       Just thinking of Gibraltar
       When she was told she hadn't oughta
       She died

       When she was told she hadn't oughta
       She fell to the ground and died
       When she was told she hadn't oughta
       She fell to the ground and died
       When she was told
       When she was told she hadn't oughta
       Told she hadn't oughta, told she hadn't oughta
       She died, she died. she died.

Jack: That's local and I'm Jack James with Jill Johns

Jill: Jill Johns with Jack James

Jack: That's local and I'm Jack James with Jill Johns

Jill: Jill Johns with Jack James

Jill: Now Jack's up
       With a report on

The Rate on Purchase
& the Balance by which
Each is judged—

Jack: The Balance of every purchase
is an average daily Balance.
Each daily Purchase
is added in the Life Cycle for, as
applicable, Purchase incurred before
The Conversion Date and Purchase incurred
on or after the Conversion Date. Each
day is begun with the opening Balance
for the Life Cycle for whatever Purchase
and all new Purchase and other
debts are added (including any posted
that day), subtracting all Payment and other
Credits posted to the Principal since the start
of the Life Cycle (including any posted
that day). The daily Balance for Purchase
incurred on or after the Conversion Date
is as follows: each day is
begun with the opening Balance for the
Life Cycle for Purchase and all New Purchase
and other debts posted to the Principal
since the start of the Life Cycle (including
any posted that day) subtracting as before
(including any posted that day). However
there is no Balance for
Purchase incurred either before or on
or after the Conversion Date in any
Life Cycle in which there is no
Previous Balance for Purchase, or in which all
Payments and Credits applied to Purchase

for the Life Cycle at least equal the
Previous Balance for all Purchase for the
Life Cycle.

Jill: Much thanks, Jack
Much to brood on
Much thanks, Jack
Much to brood on
Much thanks, Jack
Thanks much, Jack
Much thanks, Jack
Much to brood on,
Much thanks.

Jack: Now here's the story of a man

Jill: A man hit by a man

Jack: Because he wouldn't fall down

Jill: Because he fell too soon

Jack: Here's the story of a man hit by a man

Jill: Because he wouldn't fall down to his knees

Jack: Here's the story of a man

Jill: Here's the story of a man

Jack: Who fell down to his knees

Jill: So he wouldn't be hit

Jack: Because he wouldn't fall down

Jill: Fall down on his knees

Jack: Because he wouldn't fall down

Jill: Because he wouldn't fall down

Jack: Just 'cause he wouldn't fall down on his shoulders

Jill: Just 'cause he wouldn't fall down on his ears

Jack: Just 'cause he wouldn't fall down on his clothes or

Jill: Just 'cause he wouldn't fall down on his fears

Jack: Who wouldn't fall down

Jill: Never fall down

Jack & Jill: Would never fall down, down, fall down

Jack: Just 'cause he wouldn't fall down on his nose or

Jill: Just 'cause he wouldn't fall down on his face

Jack: Just 'cause he wouldn't fall down on his molars

Jill: Just 'cause he wouldn't fall down on his back

Jack: Who wouldn't fall down

Jill: Would never fall down

Jack & Jill: Would never fall down, down, fall down

Jill: Here's the story of a man

Jack: A man hit by a man

Jill: Because he wouldn't fall down

Jack: Because he fell too soon

Jill: Here's the story of a man hit by a man

Jack: Because he wouldn't fall down to his knees

Jill: Here's the story of a man

Jack: Who would never fall

Jack & Jill: Here's the story of a man hit by a man hit by a man hit by a man
Here's the story of a man hit by a man hit by a man
Here's the story of a man hit by a man
Here's the story of a man.

Scene IV – Weather

Jane: It's getting, it's really getting

John: Kinda a change, eh—

Jack: Jane Jones with weather

Jill: Whatta 'bout it, Jane?

Jane: Well, ho ho hah, Jack
Jack, ho hah hah, Jill
Well, hah hah hah, Jack
Gonna be hah hah ho, Jill
Gonna be ho hah hah, Jill
Gonna be, well gonna be
Hah hah hah
Hah hah hah
Hah

Jill: That's right, Jane!

Jack: Jane Jones with weather

Jane: Well, ho ho hah, Jill
Jill, ho hah hah, Jack
Well, hah hah hah, Jill
Gonna be hah hah ho, Jack
Gonna be ho hah hah, Jack
Gonna be, well gonna be
Hah hah hah
Hah hah hah
Hah

Jill: That's right, Jane!

Jack: Jane Jones with weather

Jane: Thanks, Jill, Jack
        It's been, it is, it's gonna be
        Thanks, Jill, Jack
        Gonna be, is, was
        Let's take a look
        Look at those pictures
        We're looking at
        Well hah hah hah hah hah
        We're looking at
        Thanks, Jill, Jack
        It's been, it is, it's gonna be
        Look at that high moving in

        Oh boy oh boy oh boy
        Let's check the radar
        Look at that, we're looking at
        Gonna be, is, was
        Take a look at that low
        Here's the five-day
        Thanks, Jill, Jack
        Is, gonna be, was
        Maybe rain, sleet, slips
        Looking at those pictures
        Check the high, looking at
        Rain, sleet, slips
        Thanks, Jill, Jack

        Beating down the coast
        Let's check the radar

Look at those highs
Wet and cold, damp and foggy
Wet and cold, damp and foggy
Beating down the coast
Let's check the radar
Look at those highs
Oh boy oh boy oh boy
Gonna be a hot one
Thanks, Jill, Jack
Gonna be a hot one
Beating down the coast
Let's check the radar
We're looking at highs in the
Gonna be a hot one
Slips, sleet, rain
We're looking at
Humid, hot and hazy
Beating down the coast
Continues wet
Let's check the radar
Here's the five-day
Looking at those pictures
Wet, wet days and swollen nights
Wet, wet days and swollen nights
Thanks, Jill, Jack
Swollen nights

It's been, it is, it's gonna be
Let's take a look
Look at those pictures
We're looking at
Well, hah hah hah hah hah hah … (cadenza)

Looking at
Wet, wet days and swollen nights
Wet, wet days and swollen nights
Moody, moody, moody

Jill: Sports is getting squeezed, Jane!
Sports is getting squeezed!
Getting squeezed, Jane!
Sports is getting squeezed!

Jane: Well, ho ho hah, Jill
Jill, ho hah hah, Jack
Well, hah hah hah, Jill
Gonna be hah hah ho, Jack
Gonna be ho hah hah, Jack
Gonna be, well gonna be
Hah hah hah
Hah hah hah
Hah

Jill: That's right, Jane!

Jane: It's getting, it's really getting

John: Kinda a change, eh—

Jack: John Jacks with the sportscast

Jill: Whatta 'bout it, John?

John: Don't go away, don't go away, don't go away

Jack: Stay with us

Jane: Well, ho ho hah, John

Jill: Don't go away, don't go away, don't go away

John: A bad day for the local teams and drug problems for a national hero.

All: We'll be right back.

Scene V – Sports

John: Twenty-eight zip
Five to three
Six-six in the third
A whopping one-eighteen to twenty-nine in overtime
Six-three, six-three, six-three in matched sets and
Four-love in the play-off
A stunning upset, a stunning upset
Clocking in a new record
Just missing that puck for a twenty-eight-twenty-seven sting
That sets the stage for next week's
Final.

And controversially
—Whaddya think of this, Jack?—
Whaddya think of this?
—Whaddya think of this, Jack?—
Star Jet Jimmy Jersey
Took up the whip
Blasting critics
"Drugs and Baseball
Are as American as
Beer and the Superbowl,"
Jousted Jersey.
"Let the drug commissioner
Get his hand
Out of his pants
Then we'll talk."
—Whaddya think of that, Jack?—
Whaddya think of that?
—Whaddya think of that, Jack?—

Jersey risks the Jets
Most severe slap
Of public flogging
If found wanting
"I love the game
Just want to stay
Even if humiliation
Is the only way."
—Whaddya think of that, Jack?—
Whaddya think of that?
—Whaddya think of that, Jack?—

Nick hits Dick
Dick throws fit
Hip-hop and a twirl
A swooping carousel of speedy sells it's prime-time
A's high, Bill's dive
Met's lurch to fixed bets
Then blow it in the trade-offs
A stunning upset, a stunning upset
Snapping in a blue escort
Just copping that slug in a million dollar tub
That wets the way, that wets the way
For next week's
Strike.

Scene VI – Closing

Jill: Geeze, Jack, we're outta time

Jack: Geeze, Jill, we're outta time

Jill: Much thanks, Jack, Jane, John

Jack: Much thanks, Jill, Jane, John

All four: Gotta go, gotta go, gotta go, gotta go
Gotta go, gotta go, gotta go, gotta go

Jill: La, la, la, la, la, la, la, la, la

Jack: La, la, la, la, la, la, la, la

Jill: Tune in tomorrow night

Jack: Tune in tomorrow night

All four: *(alternating)*

Jane: Gonna be a hot one, gonna be a cold one

Jill: Thanks for watching, thanks for watching

Jack: Have a good night, have a safe night

John: Gotta go, gotta go

All four: *(together)*

Jill: I'm Jill Jill Jill Jill Jill Jill Jill Johns

Jane: I'm Jane Jane Jane Jane Jane Jane Jane Jones

John: I'm John John John John John John John John Jacks

Jack: I'm Jack Jack Jack Jack Jack Jack Jack James

John: Tune in tomorrow night

Jane: Well, hah hah hah ho ho ho, John

John: Well, hah hah hah ho ho ho, Jane

Jane: Well, ho ho ho hah hah hah, John

John: Well, ho ho ho hah hah hah, Jane

All four: Gotta go, gotta go, gotta go, gotta go
Gotta go, gotta go, gotta go, gotta go

Jane: La, la, la, la, la, la, la, la, la

John: La, la, la, la, la, la, la, la

Jane: Tune in tomorrow night

John: Tune in tomorrow night

All four: *(alternating)*

Jane: Gonna be a hot one, gonna be a cold one

Jill: Thanks for watching, thanks for watching

Jack: Have a good night, have a safe night

John: Gotta go, gotta go

All four :   *(together)*

Jill: I'm Jill Jill Jill Jill Jill Jill Jill Johns

Jane: I'm Jane Jane Jane Jane Jane Jane Jane Jones

John: I'm John John John John John John John John Jacks

Jack: I'm Jack Jack Jack Jack Jack Jack Jack James

Together: Tune in tomorrow night

CURTAIN

The Subject

Cast

Jenny Midnight — Mezzo-Soprano
the Subject

Dr. Boris Frame — Baritone
Psychoanalyst, the Frame Institute

Professor Daemon Dudley — Tenor
Director of Social Correction
Center for Normalcy

Scene I

Scene: *Office. The Psychoanalyst (BF) sits behind an elevated wide desk in background. The Subject (JM) sits straight up on couch in foreground, facing outward (with back to desk).*

1. The Crystal Desk

Jenny Midnight [JM]:

> There's a bridge
> I can't cross
> melting like a
> boy with pickled
> eyes. She breaks
> the board over
> the crystal desk
> embodied with hieroglyphic
> inscriptions then hides
> under the folds
> of the tears
> mumbling about frozen
> papaya and the
> boat to Tonawanda.

Dr. Boris Frame [BF]:

> Uh-huh, I see, go on

JM: The sundeck collapses
> & I fall
> into a tumble

though my eyes
never knocked before
it's so thick
like molasses or
foam, the door's
been moved, I
can't recognize my
reflection.

BF: Uh-huh, I see, go on
yeah sure, ah, interesting
go on

JM: A lion
barks a familiar
song but I
don't follow the
lines of his thought.
Is that because
the powerlines are
broken or did
the repairman
warn that
this was happening?

BF: Okay, okay, okay
I see, so interesting, go on

JM: I get on
a boat — it's
crimson in the front
and swirling in the back
twisting in the back

blurring in the back
but I can't
find the mess
hall & the captain
shouts at me
to pull over.

BF: Uh-huh, I see, go on
yeah, interesting, go on
go on

JM: The light is
too dim to
make out much
else until I'm
shaking in my
bed which is
in the middle
of a pool
of soapy water.
I keep coming
but nobody touches
me. I keep
looking for the
lighthouse but I
only see holes.

BF: Lighthouse, ah-ha
I see well I see
Only yeah sure
Holes hmm so
Sure looking hmm
Well well pool

Yes touches, hole
Ah yes coming
coming, hmm, hmm

(looks at watch:)

well, yes, yes
time, now, well
time now, hmm, hmm

2. Scheduling Duet

(JM now turns toward BF for the first time)

BF: Next week's not good, Jenny
Next week's not good

JM: Not good, Dr. Frame?

BF: No good …

JM: No good …

Together: Next week's not good

BF: How about?

JM: About, about?

BF: Next Wednesday

JM: Wednesday

BF: Wednesday

JM: But I'm working, Dr. Frame

BF: How about 12:30?

JM: But I'm working, Dr. Frame

BF: Next Wednesday at 12:30

Together: Gotta switch, gotta switch, gotta switch

JM: Can't get off work, Doctor
Can't get off work

BF: Just for the month, Jenny
Just for the month, Jenny

JM: I'm not sure …

BF: Don't be sure …

JM: Is there time? …

BF: Always time …

JM: I'm not sure …

BF: Just decide

JM: I'm not sure …

BF: Can't get off? …

*

JM: Next week's not good, Doctor
Next week's not good

BF: Not good, Jenny, then?

JM: No good …

BF: No good …

Together: Next week's not good

JM: How about?

BF: About, about?

JM: Next Friday

BF: Friday

JM: Friday

BF: But I'm working all day Friday

JM: How about 2:30?

BF: But I'm working, Dr. Frame

JM: Next Friday at 2:30

Together: Gotta switch, gotta switch, gotta switch

JM: Can't get off work, Doctor —
Next week's not good.

BF: Just for the month, Jenny.
Just for the month, Jenny.

JM: Nothing settles

BF: Nothing settled

Together: Nothing settles, nothing settled

BF: Okay, okay, what now?

(Dr. Frame is blacked out, spotlight on Jenny Midnight.)

3. JM's Elegy

JM *(turns again outward)*:

> When I was a girl
> I fell down
> I looked out the window
> And saw the lake there
> I saw the rain
> When I was a child
> I wept, I crept, I slipped
>
> Everywhere I look I see people
> staring at me. I try to
> hide. The boulders are too
> big in Montana, but there
> is a voice that tells me
> to go to sleep — nothing
> is right. When I was a
> boy my mother told me. Now
> I just keep quiet.

When I was on fire
I lay down
I looked out the flames
And saw the haze there.
I saw the rain
When I was a twirl
I spun, I spun, I spun.

When I was a toy
my father spun me
around. I try to lie.
The boulders are too
big in Alabama, but there
is a force that makes me
slow to reach — nothing
fits right. When I was a girl
my father'd hold me. Now
I just keep quiet.

BF: Uh-huh, uh-huh, uh-huh

4. Frame's Analysis

BF (in reply, gets up from his chair and walks toward JM, coming into the light spotting her, which slowly widens to include them both):

The world has no conclusions
Jenny
I can no more face your pain
Than play music I never learned
Hard to listen, harder to turn
A fate into a charm
Our thoughts undo

The first as tragedy
The second as dew
The cry I hear is not the one you say
But another hidden deep away
(Don't fear the cry that
Hides so deep away)
This swirl has no conclusions
For all its protrusions,
Contusions, delusions, and shame

So many masks that cast a pall
Upon those singular calms
You cannot recall

That jag you as toy or top
Unwanted friend, untwisted bend, unfinished end
Thrown back to your unchosen fund
That lulls you at edge of come
Unrighted wrong, unspoken song, untouched too long

This will come to end, Jenny Midnight:
If you bear through the drama
To where seam breaks seam
And split the tide
Became you to become the thing
You dream
But not tonight, Jenny Midnight
Not tonight
Don't fade into alarm
Or call the ghosts
Against the swarm
Not tonight Jenny Midnight
Not tonight

(JM and BF side by side):

JM: Then try to learn this music
Listen to what I can't say
Teach me music I never played

BF: Hard to listen, harder to turn
A fate into a charm

JM: A fate into a charm

Together: Our thoughts undo
The first as tragedy
The second as dew

BF: The cry I hear is not the one you say
But another hidden deep away

Together: Don't fear the cry that hides so deep away.
This swirl has no conclusions
For all its protrusions
Contusions, delusions, and shame

(BF and JM together):

BF: This will come to end —
Jenny Midnight
Having torn through the harder
To where dream fakes dream
And knit the slide —

Don't blame, no shame, make your mark
It's just not right

Just hold on tight

Not tonight, Jenny Midnight
Not tonight

(together):

JM: When I was a top
I spun down
I looked in the mirror
And saw my hate there
I saw the pain
When I was a lock
I came, I came, I came

Everywhere I look I see people
caring for me. I have my
pride. Your shoulders are too
big for my enclosures, but there
is a choice that won't let me
glow in heat. Turn on
the lights, Dr. Frame,
turn on the lights!

BF: Jenny, we need more time

JM: I'm just drained, Dr. Frame

BF: Don't fade away

JM: I'm just not right, Dr. Frame

BF: We'll meet next week

JM: Can't take more pain

BF: You'll be fine

JM: I've got no fight

BF: We need more time

JM: There's so much fright, Dr. Frame

BF: Things will be all right
     You'll be all right

5. Jenny's Platform

JM *(increasingly agitated, obsessive; stands up and paces)*:

> People should love and approve of me.
> Making mistakes is terrible.
> People should be called on their wrongdoings.
> It's horrible when things go wrong.
> I can't control my emotions.
> Threatening situations keep me worried.
> Self-discipline is too hard.
> The bad effects of my childhood still control my life.
> I can't stand the way most people act:
> avoiding responsibility
> terribly unfair
> demanding your attention or
> abusive
> afraid of their own worthlessness
> angry
> bored

lonely
paralyzed
helpless
hopeless …

JM and BF: People should love and approve of me.
Making mistakes is terrible.
People should be called on their wrongdoings.
It's horrible when things go wrong.
I can't control my emotions.
Threatening situations keep me worried.
Self-discipline is too hard.
The bad effects of my childhood still control my life.
I can't stand the way most people act
Angry — bored — lonely — paralyzed — helpless — hopeless

6. Normalcy

(Light goes up on Frame, who is sitting at his desk.)

BF *(from desk)*: Are you a normal person, Jenny Midnight?
Probably for the most part you are.
Your sex complexes, your fears and hatreds, your furies and deceptions, all your anger and your spite

all normal
absolutely normal
it's normal
couldn't be more normal.

JM: That's normal —

BF: I can still remember
vividly the fear I once experienced, as a child,
when threatened, on the way to school,
by a half-witted boy with an air-gun.
But a person who calls himself a psychologist
is in a peculiar position these days. Experiments
show that Norway rats
die quickly if their whiskers are clipped
and they are thrown into
tanks of water.

JM: That's normal —

BF: In fact,
we have two emotional levels, one
fundamental and the other more or less
superficial.
In fact,
most people need only a few close
friends, with a larger circle
of casual friends.

And this is normal
100 percent normal.

JM: It's normal —

BF: But if someone says these
things to a man on his way to the office,
sometimes he can scarcely do his work
and will go home to bed.
In such an atmosphere
a husband can develop a disturbing
sense of inferiority.

He begins
to doubt that he still has the capacity
to be attractive. He may
become so convinced that he has lost his
charm that he no longer
makes any effort to look nice or
appear charming.

JM: And this is normal —

BF: Men like to be bossed.
Men are fearful. Glandular
differences make them five times more fearful
than women. They attach far more
importance to security than women do;
as a result, they need
constant reassurance.

And this is normal
completely normal.

JM: It's normal —

BF: But some parents
always act
protective toward their children
not thinking
that by killing
their nerve they are also killing their chances
of having rich,
exciting, and successful lives. Children
are born with
practically no fears and if not repressed
by their overanxious and tyrannical

parents
would have a natural courage that would
sustain them throughout the rest of their lives.

And this is normal
absolutely normal.

Nor can I second
your notion that
you've got moral grounds for divorce. Rather,
I think your
misery calls …

JM: My misery calls …

BF: … for continued treatment.

You see, Jenny
many people have trouble
with everyday activities
such as
Speaking, thinking, caring

JM: Forbearing

BF: Walking, sleeping, dining

JM: Reclining

BF: Singing, talking, crying

JM: Replying, moping, coping

BF: Hoping, mopping
Playing, dreaming, sharing

JM: Repairing

BF: Waiting, clinging, whining

JM: Rewinding

BF: Hopping, skipping, lying

JM: Denying, beating
      Faking, sliding

BF: Eating, drinking
      Yawning, shrieking

Together: Hiding

And this is normal
All this is normal
Couldn't be more normal

A crutch
shares the weight of burden
protecting without shielding
but should not be used
without specific instruction

BF: Slurping, vying

JM: Spilling, swelling

Together: Searching

Together: Nothing settles, nothing settled

Interlude. BF and JM dance to "The Introjection Tango."

Scene II

Scene: The same. Knocks are heard. Prof. Daemon Dudley enters and joins BF behind the desk, creating the impression of a trial. The Subject is seated upright facing the examiners.

1. The Inquisitor

Prof. Daemon Dudley [DD]:

> Which best describes your dress size? What brands of bar soap have been used in your household in the past 6 months? Which of the following hypoallergenic products are currently being used in your household? Which of the following best describes the sensitivity of your skin? To which of the following products have you experienced a negative reaction? On average, how many days per week do you use foundation? Do you use a facial cleanser other than bar soap?
>
> Do you, Jenny, do you?
>
> Do you or anyone in your family wear support pantyhose? What brands of underwear do you wear? Do you own an automatic dishwasher? If so, how many loads do you do in your automatic dishwasher in an average week? Do you use Mexican sauces such as salsa or picante?
>
> Do you, Jenny, do you?
> Well, do you, Jenny, do you?

(to BF) No response, no reply, not a word
Affect is poor, prognosis dim

BF: When you hammer there's no gain
I have better methods to undo her pain

(to JM): But won't you tell what's in your mind
Something in which we might find
A clue for Dr. Dudley?

2. Songs of Crossed Purposes

JM: The house is empty
Nor can I see
What beholds me
As I walk in the dusk
Of a storm that breaks
Over and over against
My evasions
Or glimpses of what
I have held too long

I'm stumbling
I'm fumbling
I'm suffering, Dr. Frame

Touch fails
I can find no way
In the emptiness
That surrounds me—
The cost of the passage
The weariness of my exposures

I'm stumbling
I'm fumbling
I'm suffering

Nothing holds
Against what promise
Impales itself on
Loss — my eyes
Burn in vain
For what I know
In faith I
Never had
Eyes like your eyes
As if you might balance
Broken scales
Reverse the charm
That crushes me …
In its grip

I'm stumbling
I'm fumbling
I'm suffering, Dr. Frame

DD: The principle of the surround, Ms. Midnight
      is the destiny of the found —
      like grace will hold a pattern only so long

      So —
      quantify your regard, the sequence of your fall
      as tall as or trips to the kitchen or
      for instance, Ms. Midnight, the length of time
      from the last time to
      this
      or say the color of the rope or the size of the
      slope?
      Or say the color or the size of the slope?

3. Men's Talk

DD *(to BF)*: She's all yours.
I'm only interested
In the classification of disorder:
I can see no special case here
Only more evidence to compile.

BF: State the case and the case refuses.

DD: The importance of psychology
In obtaining a tangible psycho-neural
Hypothesis of emotion
Can hardly be exaggerated.

BF: You stare into a void of your projection
Locked on a constant as if it were a star

DD: There is distinct evidence
Of a baffled or thwarted element that creeps
Into the subject's reaction
As the emotion proceeds to its climax.

BF: Your climax, Professor
The jimmy you hammer on like a bobbing
Dragon at a quixotic funeral
Rummaging for harnesses in a boardroom of squirrels

DD: Say what you will, but
Normal minds never run adrift
When there are no environmental factors to poison them.

BF: The only animal completely adapted to its environment
Is a dead animal

DD: No opinions sway me
     My principles are my only guide

 BF: Principles like profit
     Honor only those who choose
     Not to honor them

DD: The totality of energy generated
     Within the junctional tissue
     Whenever the membrane is continuously energized,
     From the emissive pole of an adjacent cell
     To the receptive pole of the next,
     Intrinsically constitutes consciousness.

 BF: Consciousness of what we have forgotten
     When we refuse to
     Recall, what eludes mention, derails
     Attention. Every misstep I take
     Leads to where I
     Might yet be, the who I make

(musing to himself)

     I had felt this way myself
     Slugged by the advantage of a wantless need —
     A silver dollar or a flavored
     Buffalo nickel. As if drift could be a
     Condition not of helplessness but of
     Hope *(DD echoes)*

DD: Prediction and control, that's the game for me
     Defining the criteria
     Not letting the criteria define me
     No subject ever gets away

We always get our man
We take whatever words they say
And make them sing our song
We make them sing our song

JM: Ah …

It hurts
It weighs too much
Why are you saying this?
I'm afraid, feeling dazed, I've been used
Give me some space

4. The Subject

JM *(looking neither toward the others or the audience but in a mutter to herself):*
It hurts
It hurts
I trip
I fall
I can't remember who I am
Why do I feel this way?
I'm afraid
I've lost direction
Where is this?
How far is that?
I can't understand
Why can't things be the way they were?
I walk up and down
They keep asking me, What's wrong?
I forget where home is

It doesn't bother me
I just drift and stare
It's getting darker
It frightens me
It doesn't care what I think
Don't touch!
You'll never find me!
Let me alone!
Don't do that!
I don't belong here!
Let go of me!

(agitated, paranoid, stands, turns suddenly, and stares outward)

Better turn the radio
off, turn down
that screaming!
Why are you looking
at me like that?
I said get out
of here I told
you that scares me
turn the light back
on take your
hands off me
I said stop
shaking me
it hurts too much
put down the knife
it's not funny
I said
don't look at me
that way why are

you staring at me
that way …

(with increasing terror)

who brought me here
split me like that
turn down
that screaming
I said
stop shaking like that
your face in mine
I said get out
turn the light back
like that
what are you looking
I said
that scares
at me like
of here I told
I said like that
I said
like that

(sudden change of voice to child)

We used to have a whole bunch of bunnies
& then the last one ran away
So we got a hamster
Two hamsters we got one for my sister's birthday
We got another one and she named him Happy
for Happy Birthday
& I when I come home from school

I sometimes go out with my mom
Mommy!
Or I go to my friend's house
& have ice cream chocolate
Ice cream or we have sprinkles
Lots of sprinkles

BF: That's all for now, Jenny
     That's all for now

JM: That's all, Dr. Frame?

BF: That's all

JM: That's all

Together: That's all for now

BF: What about?

JM: About?

Together: About, about?

BF: Your prescription

JM: Prescription

BF: Prescription

JM: But I'm quitting, Dr. Frame

BF: Then how about at bedtime?

JM: But I'm quitting, Dr. Frame

BF: Every night — 10:30

Together: Gotta quit, gotta quit, gotta quit

JM: Can't get off now, Doctor
Can't get off now

BF: No more time now, Jenny
No more time now

5. Mommy [Trio]

DD *(dominant voice of the three)*:
Are you for
Bacon or pork? Bacon or pork?
Republican or GOP?
Do you watch
Tapes or TV, tapes or TV?
Do you watch
Videos or movies on TV?
Are you for
Liquid or drink? Liquid or drink?
Underwear or BVDs?
Do you like
Frozen or iced?
Cut-up or sliced?
Do you take
Valium or psychotherapy?

BF: Uh-huh, I see, go on
Uh-huh, I see, go on
Go on, yeah sure, okay

JM: Why don't you leave me alone
O, leave me alone
O, why can't you let me be
O, leave me alone
O, leave me alone
O, won't you let me stay here with my mommy
Somebody call my mommy

All three: Gotta quit, gotta quit, gotta quit
No more time now
Nothing settles, nothing settled
(DD:) Then it's settled

BF: Jenny, there's no more time.

6. *The Children Are Quiet, the Horses Merry, & Everyone's Gone to Sleep (Subject's Valediction)*

JM *(to BF)*: Time's up, okay, goodbye

(stands, faces forward):

It's a stone's throw from yesterday
& I already regret tomorrow
I'm afraid
But already forget what
I'm afraid of

I'll take a turn
to tune the time
or trip by bits
and crawl upon
a spattered floor.

Just take a turn
to time the tune
or trip the slips
and fall upon
a rusted door.

Turns that guide me
or gorge —
Spin me round a
tree of tumbled
call or wait
till tongues break
over backs that clatter.

A stone's throw from yesterday
but the mind knows —
but the mind knows —
Spin me round
spin me round, spin me round.
I'm afraid
but already forget what
I'm afraid of
I already forget what
I'm afraid of.

Now I just keep quiet.

(Jenny exits and the next subject enters, replacing her in the patient's chair.)

CURTAIN

The Lenny Paschen Show

Cast

Lenny Paschen — the Kamikaze King of Comedy — Baritone

Monica Moolah — Rising Star — Soprano

Paul Evangeline — Crossover Singer — Tenor

Maria Aquavita — Show Business Legend — Mezzo-Soprano

Bud Dickie — Ventriloquist's Dummy

Les Lulling & his band

All action takes place on the television studio set of a late night talk show. There are two stage areas for the set: a panel area with Lenny's desk and four guest seats to his right, and a performance area next to the onstage band. Bud Dickie starts at curtain in the seat next to Lenny and is moved over by each new guest.

Scene I

(*Theme music*)

Announcer (*off-stage*):

Live from high atop New York's incredulous Upper West Side, it's the Lenny Paschen Show. Lenny's guests tonight are show biz legend Maria Aquavita, singing sensation Paul Evangeline, and the sparkling and irrepressible Monica Moolah. & featuring Bud Dickie & the music of Les Lulling & his combo. & now, ready or not, the Kamikaze King of Comedy, take it & mangle it, Lenny!

(*Lenny comes out to the stage area.*)

Lenny: Fuck you.
Or let me put it this way:
Good evening ladies & gentlemen
& fuck you!
You think that's funny?
Give you a tickle?
Give you a chuckle?
Give you a laugh?
Ha ha ha ha, ha ha ha.

Let me tell you something else:
Fuck you.
And fuck the asshole sitting next to you.
Fuck both of you.

Morons.
You're a bunch of morons.
Especially the asshole sitting next to you.
Or the one you're sitting on.
Ha ha ha ha, ha ha ha.

Idiots.
Zombies.
Stupidos.
Intellectually challenged.
Comprende?

Let me tell you something else.
You and your family
& a quarter
Won't buy a cup of coffee
At Woolworth's.
So fuck you,
& the people you came here with.

Five years.
Five lost years we've been
Giving it to you
On most of these same stations.

You want to hear something funny?
I'll tell you something funny:
Like the one about the guy—

Like the one about the guy—
Like the one about the guy—
Drops dead on his way to the show.
Like the one about the guy—
Like the one about the guy—
Like the one about the guy—
Spills his guts out to a bunch of dummies.
I'm talking about Americans—
The aesthetically challenged people.

Suburbanites, exburbanites,
Suburban -urban, -urban, -urban, -urbanites.
Some urban fights, some urban rites,
Some urban, urban, urban, urban flights,
Suburbanites.

You folks couldn't tell the difference
Between an idea and a piece of
Shit
If the shit was wrapped in
Plastic and had a brand name.
Shit brand shit.
Number one in sales.
Number one in critical acclaim.
Rated by *The New York Times*,
The *Village Voice*, and *People* magazine
As the number one shit.

You want to hear something funny?
I'll tell you something funny:

My humor is so dark you can't see it.
You think that's funny?

Give you a ha ha ha ha
Ha ha ha ha ha ha ha ha.
Fuck you, fuck you.

Morons.
You're a bunch of morons.
Did you people forget
To put your brains in
This morning?

Oh, my God, my God
I'm out here all alone.

It's over. It's over.
I'm a dead schmuck.
Over & out.

Fade to black, fading to black.
Nobody out there.
Blankity blank blank blank.
Nobody out there.
I'm all alone in front of you.
I'm a dead Jew
yakking to a bunch of stiffs.

(spoken)

Oh boy, oh boy, oh boy.
Tonight we've got
an incredible line-up:
the vocal stylings of Paul Evangeline
Knockout newcomer Monica Moolah
& my very dear friend
& a friend of us all

Maria Acquavita.
Les Lulling is here with the band.
Hit it Les!

(Lenny moves to his desk in the panel area of the set.)

Lenny: Total washout.
Boy, did I blow it.
They killed me.
Now I'm in deep shit
Up to my Adam's apple.

(turns to Bud Dickie)

But I've always got my
Dickie to play with, right?
Like if your date says goodnight
A guy's got to find his own friends.
You folks all know my better half,
Bud Dickie—Buddy, Dickie,
Say hello to the folks at home.

Bud *(Lenny in falsetto)*:

Hello, folks, and
Ain't this a terrible show?

Lenny: Dickie, Dickie, you're a son of a bitch.

Bud: Whatever you say, Lenny,
Whatever you say.

Lenny: Dickie, Dickie,
My favorite fat boy.

Bud: Well, I never turn
Down a piece of pie,
If that's what you mean.

Lenny: Dickie, Dickie,
You're a pig in a suit.

Bud: What can I say? Lenny,
What can I say?
Someday I'd like to give you
A piece of my mind.
But I'm afraid you wouldn't
give it back, give it back, give it back!

Lenny: I should have fired you years ago.

(*turns to audience*)

What's the matter with you?
What's the matter with you?
Did your wife shove your face in a Cuisinart?
You never looked so blue.

Nothing better to do?
Nothing better to do?
Go stick your head in a microwave
Till there's nothing left but goo.

Sometimes we all need a friend
Someone to see us round the bend
Someone who's always there
To push us down the stair
Or out the door, into the cold night air.

You want to sniff some glue?
I do, do you?
Then hit ourselves with a two-by-four
Till we know what's true.
Did your wife shove your face in a Cuisinart?
Did your kids cut out the doggie's heart?
Did your father cook your mother in the stew?
Oh won't you tell me please,
What's the matter with you?

All right, let me check my cards here
Ah yeah, yeah, all right
Our first target tonight
It says right here,
Monica Moolah,
Whose hit song, "Stickin' with the Stuff"
Was premiered on our show
Won't you join me in welcoming
Monica Moolah.

(Monica enters squeezing a perfume atomizer in the direction of the au-dience and then toward Lenny as she takes her seat at the panel area.)

Monica: Lenny, Lenny,
Lenny, Lenny, Lenny
I get so
Nervous
I tell you
Lenny, Lenny,
I just can't tell you how
Nervous I get

Lenny: Monica, darling
What a sweetheart,
What a talent,
What a dreamboat.

Monica: Oh, Lenny, Lenny,
Lenny, Lenny, Lenny
I love your show.

Lenny: Monica, darling
What a twinkle
Not a wrinkle
Monica, Monica, Monica
Such a twinkle
Not even one wrinkle
Monica, Monica, Monica, Monica

Monica: Lenny, Lenny, Lenny
I don't know what to say
So great to see you.
So great to be here
So great to be anywhere.

Lenny: The way you look
Your hair, your eyes
Your everything.

Monica: My whole career, really
I've got to say this
I have you to thank,
I have you to thank, really
I've got to say this
My whole career.
I love you, Lenny

You know I love you
I really love you, Lenny
Lenny, Lenny, Lenny, Lenny.

Lenny: Monica, darling
How 'bout a number?
Sing something pretty,
How 'bout a song?

Monica: Me, who me, do a number?
A number, a musical number?

Lenny: Please, sweetheart, please
Do a number just for me.

Monica: Just for you
Well, OK

(walks over to stage area)

Lenny *(spoken)*: Ladies & gentlemen, what a treat!
Ladies & gentlemen, Monica Moolah!

Wherever Angels Go

Oh, hey, buddy, can you spare me a dime?
I've been searching for you so long
Yeah, hey, sister, I ain't into no crime
Won't you show me the way to go home

Say, hey, mister, can you help me to find
Some kind of place I can call my own?
Yo, hey, mister, I'm caught in a bind,

I'm here out on the street all alone

Been a long time, been a long time
Don't you know I've missed you so
Wherever angels go
I will take you there to glow

Oh, hey, buddy, will you spare me some time?
I've been searching for you so long.
There is no climb
Makes no difference no mind
Wherever angels go

Oh, hey, buddy, can you spare me a dime?
I've been searching for you so long
Yeah, hey, sister, I ain't into no crime
Won't you show me the way to go home
Won't you show me the way to go home

(Monica returns to panel.)

Lenny (*spoken*): Boy, that's something.
I had no idea.
Jesus, Jesus, Jesus —
show me the way to go home!

(Lenny looks over to wings.)

What's that, Jack?
All right then, we'll be right back
Right back!
Watch with me!

(blackout)

Scene II

Lenny: We're back with
         Monica Moolah & now
         Our next guest
         Needs no introduction
         You all know
         Please won't you welcome
         A fantastic performer
         & truly
         Really & truly
         How can I say this?
         A great human being
         I mean a man dripping with
         Humanity
         Join me now in giving
         A special greeting to
         Paul Evangeline, Paul Evangeline,
         Paul Evangeline.

(Paul enters the stage area. He carries a guitar.)

Paul: I wrote this song
        For a little girl
        Named Mary or Molly or Millie
        or Minnie or Mimi or
        Monica
        I wrote this song
        For a little girl
        Named ——

        She knows just who she is
        & what she means to me.

Don't Get Me Wrong

Don't get me wrong
I'm never right
Busted up and feelin' slight
The hay's in the hayloft
My monkey's bent and sore
But still I'm mad to see you
Slumping at the door

Tools are good for fixing things
My life's beyond repair
Picked a pomegranate
And I sold it to a bear
I've had enough of wanting things
I never wanted before
Please give me fifty dollars
Or I'll fall right through the floor.

Too much is gone
And what remains
Don't rate a faded scrawl
Ain't worth a crocodile's crawl.
I've had enough of this and that
Of what and who and all

Dead tired in the morning
Almost gone by night
Yet there you are
Plain as rain
Hiding in the door

Don't get me wrong
I'm never right

Hunted down and reeling like
Just like a rule that's bust its score
Just like a rule that's bust its score
But still I'm mad to see you
Pulling at the chord
Yes, still I'm mad to see you
Don't say goodbye no more.

(Monica leaves panel and walks over for duet with Paul.)

Let's Remember to Dance

Monica: Remember your first glance?
You wouldn't give me a chance
I was just a tramp to you
No way to make it through
& though you love the word
You had no words for me.

Paul: Remember that first night?
How you looked so pale with fright
Yet soon you made me see
What was mean in me.

Paul & Monica: So let's remember to dance
While the world spins wild
And though our feelings lie
Let's remember to dance.

Paul: We've both known better days
No use denying our old ways
But I know if I have faith in you
Then that one thing

Will sure come true.
And then the rage will die
And all this pain subside.

Monica: Remember the starlight
How it cut right through the night
Yet soon you made me see
All that's dark in me.

Paul & Monica: So let's remember to dance
While the world spins wild
And though our feelings lie
Let's remember to dance

Truth is light
And light is glue
That holds me tight
So tightly glued to you.
Truth is light
And light is glue
That holds me tight to you.

Monica: I've seen the way
Of those that stray
Between flesh and spirit,
Spirit's made as flesh in you.

Paul: I've seen the way
Of those that stray
Between flesh and spirit,
Spirit's made as flesh in you.

Paul & Monica: So let's remember to dance
While the world spins wild
And though our feelings lie
Let's remember to dance

Lenny (*spoken*): Come over here,
Paul & Monica.
Let's dance! Let's dance!

(*Paul and Monica jog back to panel. Paul hugs Lenny, kisses him on the cheek and sits to his right.*)

Paul: Lenny, your show has
Really been
I mean it's meant
It's meant really
So much
So much to all of us,
Lenny.

Lenny: It means a lot
That you come on my show
& you pay me this respect

Paul: You're the king, Lenny
Kamikaze King of Comedy

Monica: Our king

Paul: Kamikaze King of Comedy

Lenny: I'm no king
Not of this realm

My truths
Flap & flop
On these waves of air.

Paul: What is truth?
Lenny, I've got to say this
You know I'm with you
But you're too strung up still
As if our acts went beyond this show
I love your passion, Lenny
But the show's out of step
with today's sensibility.
It smacks too hard
with its anger and hostility.
I love your passion, Lenny,
But the show's out of line.
Like they say in L.A.
If you're not part of the meeting
You're part of the problem.

Lenny: For a thirty share
You'd tear out your father's eyes
& fuck your mother in the ass
I'd rather play the back room bars
Than take meetings with the scum
That own you.

Paul: Your politics is the way you live
Not just what you say
You want to change America,
You want to change America,
But you can't even change yourself,

They say it downtown too—
If you can't talk turkey
Don't talk.

Lenny: Gobble, gobble, gobble, gobble.

Monica: They can cancel you, Lenny
But they can't cancel what you are
In my heart you're still
A prince and shining star,
In my heart you'll always be
A prince and shining star.

Lenny: What's happening's
Gonna happen
Let the flips flap
Where they may
This is what I have to do
This is what I have to say.

Monica & Paul: Where you go, Lenny
We'll be right next to you
Through warp and woof
And wet and wind and wind
Eternity's not long enough
For faith, our faith, is blind,
Our faith is blind,
Our faith is blind.

Lenny: How dull you are
How slow to understand
Or can't you bear to hear
The demons you command?

You work from nine to five
Come home & watch your shows
Piling sugar on lies
Mystification on hate.
You're just a viewer to be skewered
A john to be fleeced
Don't pity me
Pity yourselves

I am not pierced
My body does not smell
But why have you forsaken
All you cannot sell?
Go on, go on
Turn the station
Let your mind become a void
What you don't figure out
Robs heaven and earth as well.

How dull you are
How slow to comprehend
Or can't you bear to hear
The demons you defend?
Don't pity me
Pity yourselves
No, don't pity me
Pity yourselves.

(*spoken*) We'll be right back
after these words from our sponsor.

(*blackout*)

Scene III

Lenny: We're back and we've got
One more guest for you
Please won't you join me
In welcoming
The entirely enticing
Maria Aquavita

(*Maria comes out and sits at the panel.*)

Maria: Lenny, Lenny, Lenny, Lenny

Lenny: Maria, Maria Aquavita, Maria,
so happy to see ya.

Maria: Lenny, Lenny,
Lenny, Lenny, Lenny,
You've got to lighten up
Unfasten your shoes.
You're about as uptight
As a bed of screws.
I've listened to all you've had to say
I hear your grandiloquent blabber—
All your talk of things that matter.
Yet somehow you've lost touch
With what was once
As plain as sense.
There's more to art than echoes
Caterwauling against events.
There's more to art than jelly
Shimmying as if it meant.
You talk incessantly

And the blasts hit and
Stutter and scream
But it's only explosions of steam.

I know the pain
I know the price
I've been there
More than once or twice,
I've been there
More than once or twice.
Till I was nothing but
A broken mirror
Shattered into shards
And all the pieces
Don't add up
They don't add up
Not even to a
Pack of cards.
I know the pain
Just like you
The dagger's tooth
Of ignorance's pride.
I know the pain.
I've paid the price
Of shouting in corridors
To empty rooms
Or turned backs
And bridges burned.

Reality is more
Than just what washes up on shore
Hold out your hand
And come with me

I'll take you to a place
Where things are
Just as they should be
No tyranny no more
No homeless and no poor
Hold out your hand
Go through that door
Leave the rich and powerful
To crumple to the floor
Forget this world
Come away with me
To where the desperate dance
And the scorned set free.

Lenny (*spoken*): You can sell that
    & get a twenty percent return.
    There's a pie in the sky
    & enough suckers to pay
    the one that pipes it.

Maria, Paul, & Monica (Chorus):
    The USA, the USA, there's no one stopping us now
    The USA, the USA, it's cold, so cold in the ground.

Lenny: You people are so desperate for lobotomies
    You lobotomize yourselves.
    You people are so desperate for lobotomies
    You lobotomize yourselves.
    All you want is reruns
    It's all a bunch of crap
    Pablum for the people
    It's time to take a nap
    It's time to take your nap.

Chorus: The USA, the USA, there's no one stopping us now
The USA, the USA, it's cold, so cold in the ground.

Lenny: You people are so desperate for dependency
You've lost faith in yourselves.
You people are so desperate for dependency
You've lost faith in yourselves.
You've gone so mickey-mousey
You've forgotten how to think
Just pay a hundred dollars
To go to see a shrink
Now go and see your shrink.

Chorus: The USA, the USA, there's no one stopping us now
The USA, the USA, it's cold, so cold in the ground.

Lenny: You people are so desperate for authority
You enslave yourselves.
You people are so desperate for authority
You enslave yourselves.
Sure they'll yank me off the air waves
Say I'm too obscene
'Cause I say fuck the ruling class
And you know who I mean
You know just who I mean.

Chorus: The USA, the USA, there's no use stopping us now
The USA, the USA, it's cold, so cold in the ground.
It's oh, so cold in the ground
It's cold, so cold in the ground.

Lenny, Lenny
Lenny, Lenny, Lenny

No one puts it
Better than you do
You're like a
Man-o-man-o-man
A far-out dude.

Lenny, Lenny
Lenny, Lenny, Lenny
You're a far-out dude.

The show's sensational tonight
The show's sensational tonight
Sensational, sensational, sensational
tonight, tonight.

What a hit, what a buzz
What a smash, what a gas
What a turn-on, you've got guts
What a hit, what a buzz
What a smash, what a gas
What a turn-on, you've got guts
O-man-o-man, o-man-o-man
Lenny, Lenny
Lenny, Lenny, Lenny

The show's sensational tonight
The show's sensational tonight
Sensational, sensational, sensational
Tonight, tonight.

Lenny: I won't stop
I can't surrender
With uncanny ceremony

Forsaken I forsake
For this is my come-on
And this is my bit,
I've given up everything but schtick.

(with Maria echoing:)

        I can't stop
        I won't surrender
        With flagrant defiance
        Forsaken I forsake
        They say that I'm fucked up
        They say that I'm sick
        I've given up
        everything but schtick.
        I won't stop.

Chorus: Lenny, Lenny, Lenny, Lenny.

Maria: There's an eggplant in heaven
        Seen it shine, seen it shine
        There's an eggplant in heaven
        Seen it shine
        There's an eggplant, there's an eggplant
        And it's coming, coming for us
        There's an eggplant up in heaven
        Seen it shine.

        For every trial there is an ending

Chorus: Must be time, must be time

Maria: For every trouble a dead end

Chorus: Must be time

Paul: I'd love to have a nickel

Chorus: Must be time, must be time

Paul: For every man who's called me friend.

Chorus: Must be time.

Maria: There's an eggplant in heaven

Chorus: Shines so fine, shines so fine

Maria: There's an eggplant in heaven

Chorus: Shines so fine

Maria: There's an eggplant up in heaven

Chorus: And it's coming, coming for us.

Maria: There's an eggplant in heaven

Chorus: Shines so fine.

Maria: For every gulp there is a burp.

Chorus: Must be mine, must be mine

Maria: For every rich man ten in rags.

Chorus: Must be mine.

Monica: Never trust your soulfulness

Chorus: Must be mine, must be mine

Monica: To a man who has no curves.

Chorus: Must be mine.

Chorus: There's an eggplant in heaven
Just like mine, just like mine
There's an eggplant in heaven
Just like mine
There's an eggplant up in heaven
And it's coming, coming for us
There's an eggplant up in heaven
Just like mine.

There's an eggplant in heaven
Looks like mine, looks like mine
There's an eggplant in heaven
Looks like mine
There's an eggplant in heaven
And if I can't sell it
Gonna call that eggplant turpentine
I'm gonna call that eggplant turpentine.

Lenny: Well, that about wraps up the show.
Yes, that about wraps up the show.
Thanks, Maria.
& remember to check out
Maria's new CD.
Monica & Paul will be appearing
Next month in

Milan, Kansas and
Peking City, Montana.
And Dickie & me & Les & the band
Will be back on
Most of these same stations
Real soon.

Lenny, Monica, Paul, and Maria:
Bye now, so long, take care
Even if you can't see us we'll be there
We'll be back real soon.

Lenny, Lenny, Lenny, Lenny

Bye now, so long, take care
Even if you can't see us we'll be there
We'll be back real soon.
Goodnight, goodnight, goodnight.

CURTAIN

Appendix
Lenny's Monologue: Extended Play

The three librettos I wrote for Ben Yarmolinsky in the early 1990s used vernacular American forms to create contemporary operas with a social and historical address. *Blind Witness News* (1990) and *The Lenny Paschen Show* (1992) used the typical format of late-night TV, while *The Subject* (1991) starts with a psychoanalytic session.

Lenny is the final work of the trilogy. Much of the opening monologue, presented here, was cut, for reasons of length, from the final libretto.

In its typical process of canceling sense, television is, of course, the offense to meaning that is addressed in *The Lenny Paschen Show*. Lenny Paschen is a gladiator in an electronic age — a hot fighter in a cool medium (and he may also cut against the grain of the lyric impulse within opera). Lenny is trapped from the start, yet his struggle for moral discourse makes this opera a fin des millennia version of *Die Meistersinger* — sans masters, sans paradise, all songs. Lenny seems to preach that we can get beyond the puppetry of TV personas, but as he also insists, he remains a puppet of his own devices. *The Lenny Paschen Show* uses the tools at hand, especially the tradition of black, often abrasive, comedy to explore the worlds flaunted by, and also hidden within, one of the central formats of commercial TV.

Lenny's Monologue: EP

Fuck you.
Or let me put it this way:
Good evening ladies & gentlemen
& fuck you!
Think that's funny?
Give you a tickle?
Give you a chuckle?

Give you a laugh?
Let me tell you something else.
Fuck you.
& fuck the asshole sitting next to you.
Fuck both of you.
Morons.
You're a bunch of morons.
Especially the asshole next to you.
Or the one you're sitting on.
Hardee har har har.
Idiots.
Morons.
Stupido.
Intellectually challenged.
Comprende?
Dull normal.
Let me tell you something else.
You & your family —
Or should I say viewing partners —
& a quarter
Won't buy a cup of coffee
At Woolworth's.
So fuck you.
& the people you came here with.
Five years.
Five years we've been
Giving it to you
On most of these same stations.
I'll tell you this:
If you're waiting to feel
Good about yourself
You're gonna wait 'til the
Slime that call themselves

Defenders of family values
Turn themselves in for
Pandering & prostitution &
Grand theft, humanity.
I'll tell you this:
If you're looking to feel
Good about yourself —
Hit your switch.
Tune out.
Go ahead …
Switch the station.
Put me out of my misery.
I'll tell you this —
Switch the channel
Turn on one of those
Urine-soaked white-bread sit coms
You people lap up
Like puppy chow.
Shit.
Shows guaranteed to
Deplete your intelligence
After a single viewing.
Irreversible brain rot.
Or is deplete too many
Syllables for you to follow?
Morons.
Idiots.
Stupido.
Intellectually challenged.
Comprende?
Dull normal.
You folks wouldn't know a joke
If it splattered cum all over

Your TV sets.
"Mildred, what's the white stuff
On the TV! Get me that
Jar of Windex!"
You folks
Couldn't tell the difference
Between an idea and a piece of
Shit
If the shit was wrapped in
Plastic and had a brand name.
Shit brand shit.
Number one in sales.
Number one in critical acclaim.
Rated by *The New York Times*,
The *Village Voice*, and *People* magazine
As the number one shit.
You think that's funny?
Give you a tickle?
Give you a chuckle?
Give you a laugh?
I'll tell you something funny.
I'll tell you something funny.
Fuck you.
& the people you came here with.
Especially the people you came here with.
I'll tell you something funny:
I'll tell you something funny:
Like the one about the guy —
Like the one about the guy —
Like the one about the guy —
Like the one about the guy —
Drops dead on his way to the show.
Like the one about the guy —

Like the one about the guy —
Like the one about the guy —
Like the one about the guy —
Spills his guts out
To a bunch of dummies
Bunch of dummies.
Spills his guts out
To a bunch of dummies.
I'm talking about
Americans —
Americans —
The aesthetically challenged people.
Suburbanites.
Guys in worsted plaids
And plaid worsteds
Looking to stick their dicks
In any holes won't
Talk back
& might turn a profit.
Women wearing pants suits
& jogging
Like it was a moral virtue
Stuffing themselves with
Carcinogenic fat substitutes
Just so they can be
On a program.
Like "I'm really doing something
For society because
I drink diet soda
& workout with
ThighMaster."
You want to hear something funny?
I'll tell you something funny.

I like secondary smoke.
Let me tell you something else.
Health is the greatest poison —
Self-righteousness
Makes me sick.

Boy, let me try that again.
Boy, let me try that again.

Jesus, nothing, nada.
Nada, nothing, Jesus.

My God, my god
I'm out here all alone.

Jesus —
Did you people forget
To put your brains in
This morning?
Five years & you still can't
Figure out the material.
"What's he mean, five years, Mildred?"
My humor is so dark
You can't see it.
So very dark, so very dark
You can't see it.

Boy, this is going into the toilet.
No, not the toilet. Lower down.
All the way to the sewer
& the world below.
All the way to the sewer
& the world below.

Jesus, nothing, nada.
Nada, nothing, Jesus.
All the way to the sewer
& the world below.
My humor is so dark
My humor is so dark
You can't see it
Can't see it.

It's over. It's over
I'm a dead Jew.
Over & out.
A dead Jew.
Over & out.
Fade to black, fading to black.
Sayonara Senorita.
Senorita Sayonara.
I'm staring into a void
& the void is you.
Staring into a void
& the void is you.
Nobody out there.
Blankity blank blank blank.
Nobody out there.
Blankity blank blank blank.
All alone in front of you.
I'm a dead Jew
Jacking off to a bunch of stiffs.
A dead Jew
Yakking to a bunch of stiffs.